FOLLOW
THAT CAR

For Sarah
Special thanks to Andreas Schuster,
Max Fiedler, and Paul Breuer
—S.L.

First published 2015 by Nosy Crow Ltd
The Crow's Nest, 14 Baden Place, Crosby Row
London SE1 1YW
nosycrow.com

The text type was set in AlternateGothic2 BT.
The display type was hand-lettered.

ISBN 978-0-358-21220-1

Manufactured In Malaysia
TWP 10 9 8 7 6 5 4 3 2 1
4500788093

FOLLOW THAT CAR

by **LUCY FEATHER**   illustrated by **STEPHAN LOMP**

HOUGHTON MIFFLIN HARCOURT
BOSTON   NEW YORK

Hey, you . . . yes, you!

Mouse needs **your** help and he needs it **now!**

He needs to catch Gorilla and he needs to be super-quick!

Are you ready? Then let's go!

FOLLOW THAT CAR!

Look, there's Gorilla in the yellow car, over by the café. How will Mouse catch him? See the white arrows? Can you work out which route he should follow? He certainly can't drive through that big sheet of glass, can he? But you'd better be quick — gorillas drive fast!

Uh-oh! Watch out, Mouse, this building site is busy. Look at all those tall cranes! Isn't it an exciting place? Where is Gorilla now? Can you see him? And which way should Mouse go? Why don't you follow the white arrows? Mouse will have to drive carefully, won't he? There isn't even a real road!

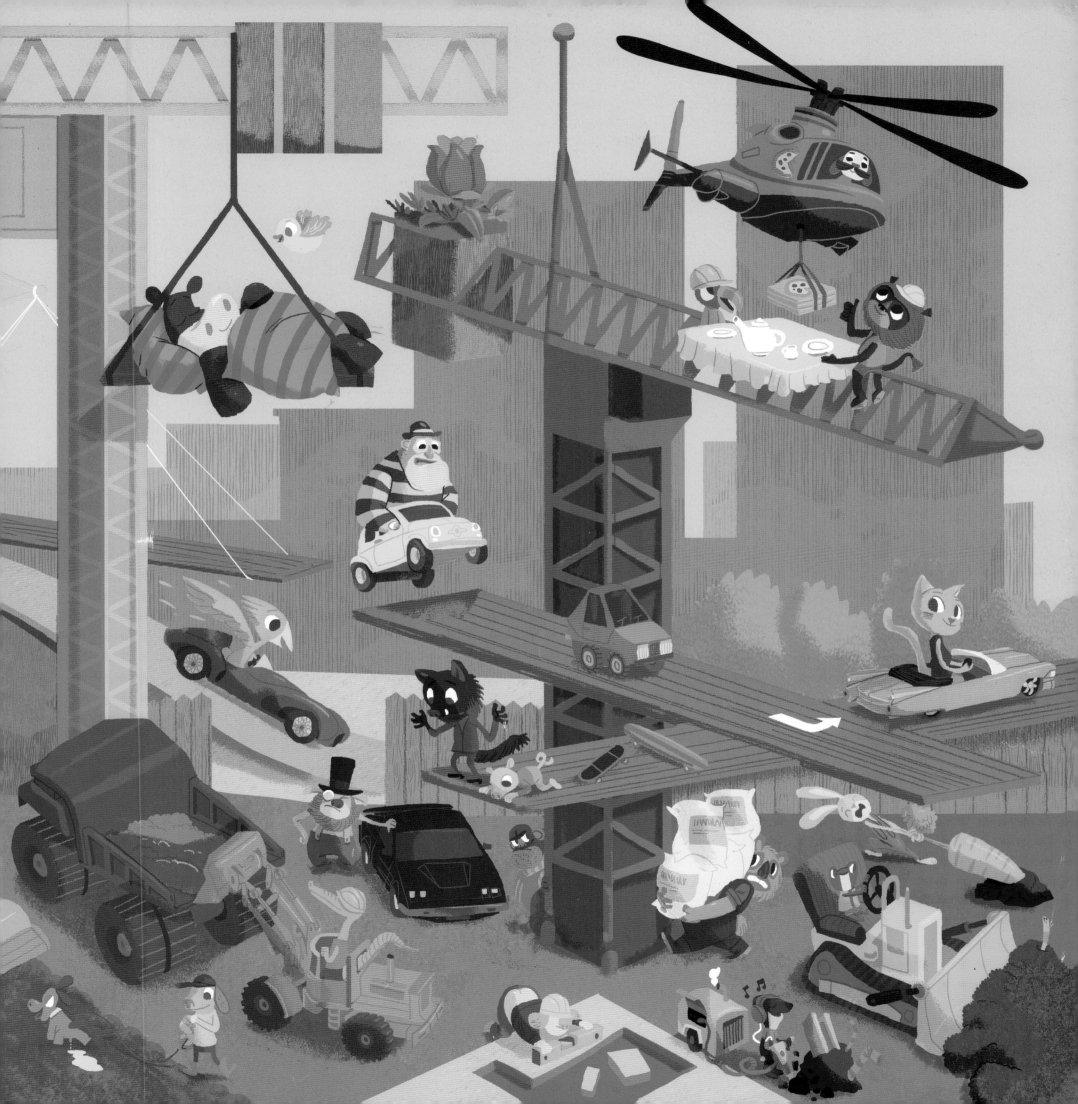

Good driving! That building site was dangerous.

Can you see Gorilla? He's so far away!

Oh dear, how is Mouse going to get through this parking garage?

He'll have to go down the ramp because that green car

is blocking the way . . . but where will he go next?

Keep moving, everyone, this mouse

is in a big hurry!

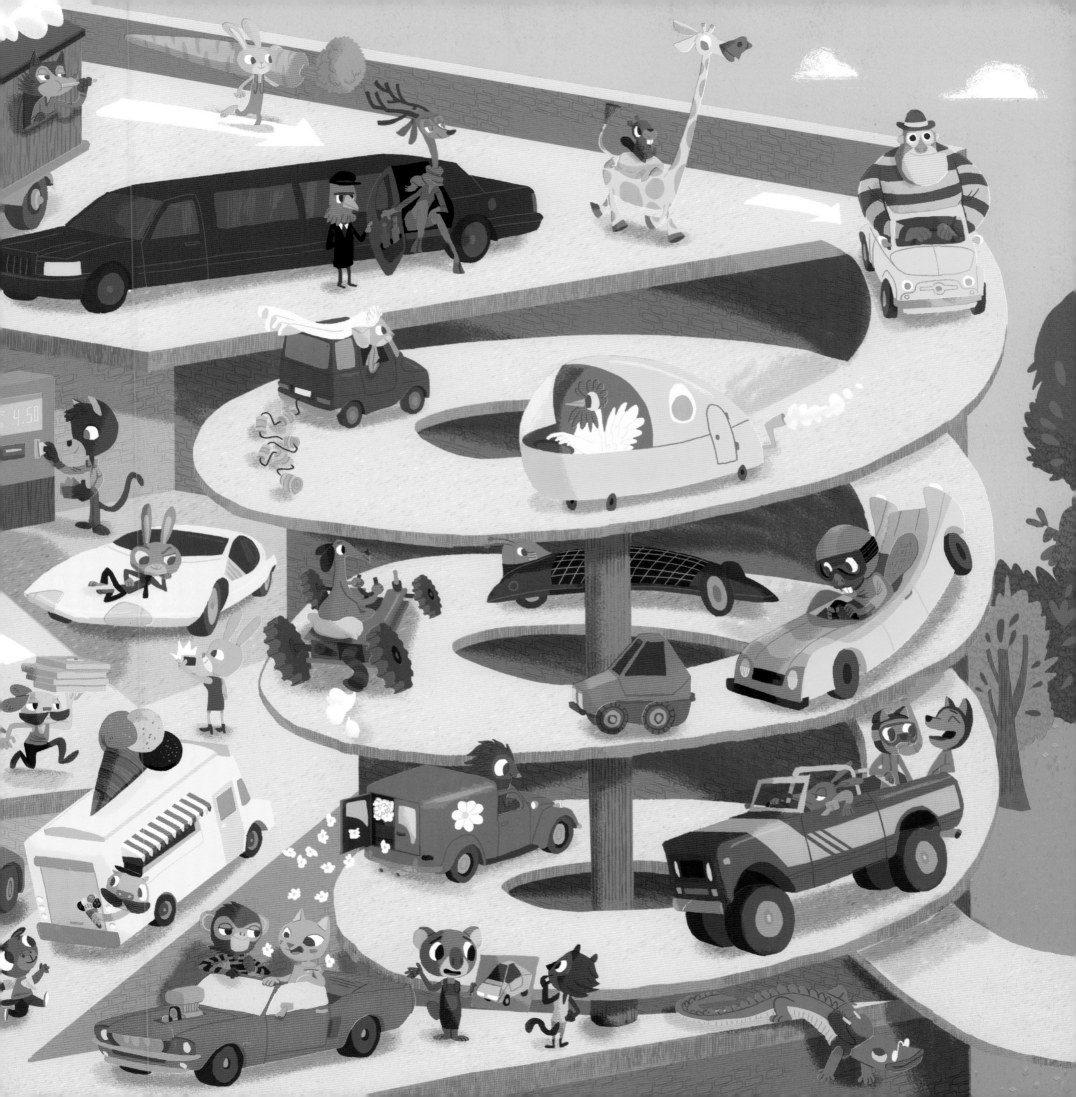

There's Gorilla!
Can you see him, too?
He's over there, by the carrots.
Oh no!
One of the roads is blocked by
a fallen tree. Mouse will have
to hurry . . . but which way
is the right way?
Don't forget those arrows!
It's a good thing you're here
to help, isn't it?

Look! Things are very busy at the train station! There are so many trains and there's a car stuck on the railroad crossing, too! Where is Gorilla now? Can you see him? There he is, looking at his map. You'll have to show Mouse which way to go. Can you spot a tunnel to take?

CIRCUS

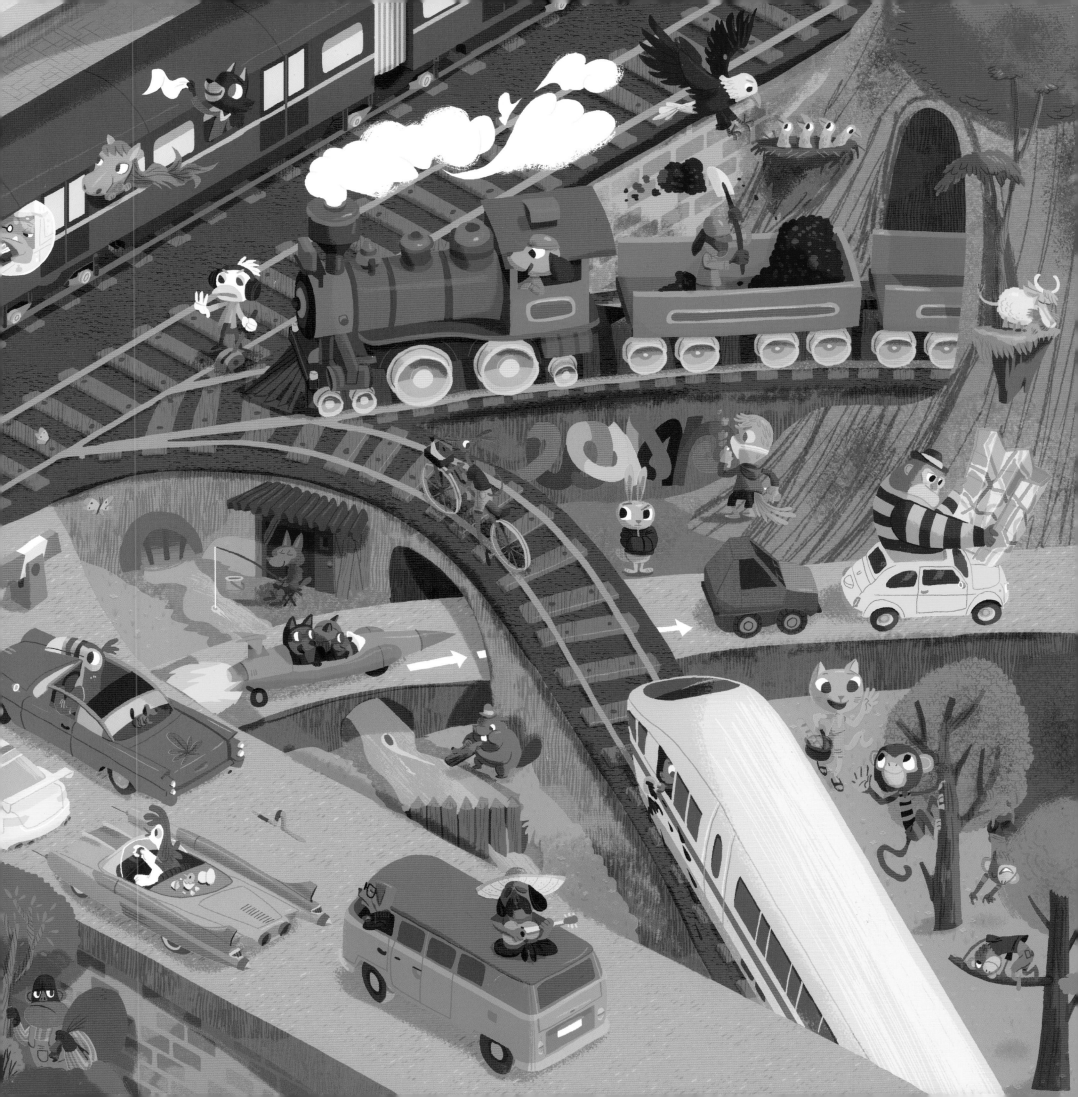

Good job
spotting that tunnel,
but Mouse still needs your help.
Gorilla's getting away! Can you see him?
Uh-oh, there's a tractor in the way,
and there are sheep everywhere, too.
If we're lucky, there might be a shortcut.
Can you find one? Quick, let's catch that
gorilla as fast as we can!

There's Gorilla!

Can you see him? He's nearly in
the mountains, and Mouse has got a very
long way to go, hasn't he? He'll have to drive through
the market, but it's full of stands and animals.
Can you help figure out which way he should go?
Just watch out for all those barrels!

Whew! These mountain roads look tough, don't they? But not for Gorilla — he's speeding away. Can you see him? But there's been an avalanche since Gorilla went past, and now Mouse can't go that way. Maybe there's another road Mouse can take? Can you find it? Be careful! The roads are very steep and slippery!

Brrr, it's chilly here, isn't it? And look where Gorilla is now!

Can you see him? Oh dear, poor Mouse is still a long, long way behind him, isn't he?

Can you help him find a way through the ski resort? He certainly can't go straight,

because there's a green truck blocking the way!

Wow! You're getting good at this, but look what's happened now! There's a traffic jam on the bridge and Gorilla has taken a shortcut. Can you see him? Let's try to catch him. Mouse will have to beep his horn to get past that red car, won't he? **BEEP! BEEP!** Watch out, Mouse, don't fall in the water!

Phew! Gorilla has stopped to get gasoline.
Can you see him? Quick, Mouse!
You can catch him now!
Can you show Mouse which is the right
bridge to cross? We'd better hurry!
Hey, Gorilla! **Stop** right now!

YOU FORGOT
YOUR BANANA!

Hooray! Gorilla has got his banana at last!
And it's all thanks to **you.**
You've been great at helping Mouse.
Come on then, everyone, it's time to go home.

But . . . oh no!

Wait, Mouse! Wait!

You dropped your cheese sandwich!

Oh dear! You'll have to help Gorilla catch Mouse.
Are **you** ready? Then let's go!

FOLLOW THAT MOTORCYCLE!